D0097423

The Mystery at Snow Lodge

New edition! Revised and abridged

By Laura Lee Hope

Illustrations by Pepe Gonzalez

Publishers · GROSSET & DUNLAP · New York

Revised and abridged by Nancy S. Axelrad.

Copyright © 1990 by Simon & Schuster, Inc. All rights reserved. Published by Grosset & Dunlap, Inc., a member of The Putnam & Grosset Book Group, New York. Published simultaneously in Canada. Printed in the U.S.A. THE BOBBSEY TWINS is a registered trademark of Simon & Schuster, Inc. Library of Congress Catalog Card Number: 88-82987 ISBN 0-448-09098-8
A B C D E F G H I J

Contents

Contents

Look for these new
BOBBSEY TWINS® reissues:

■ 1 ■
Santa's Mystery

Climbing onto the porch railing of the Bobb-seys' rambling, comfortable house, Flossie got ready to plunge into a huge snowdrift. Suddenly she stopped.

"Sleigh bells!" she squealed, clambering down onto the porch. She jumped up and down excitedly on her chubby legs, causing several strands of curly blond hair to peek out from beneath her knitted hat.

Her blond six-year-old twin, Freddie, listened to the faint jingling sound that cut through the frosty morning air. "Come on!" he called to his sister, and ran down the sidewalk.

A moment later a black horse pulling an old-fashioned sleigh came into view. Holding the reins was an old man in a heavy red jacket. On the seat behind him was a mountain of packages wrapped in pretty red-and-green paper with big shiny red ribbons on top.

1

"He looks like Santa Claus!" Freddie exclaimed as the wind blew the man's white hair in a cloud about his head.

The sleigh had a high curved back and low sides painted black. The seat upholstery and runners were all bright red.

Halfway down the block, the driver stopped in front of a house. He selected several gifts from the rear of the sleigh and trudged through the snow to the back door.

"Why is Santa bringing presents now?" Flossie asked her brother. "It isn't Christmas yet."

"But it will be soon," Freddie replied, counting on his fingers. "Christmas will be here in less than a week!"

Heavy snowstorms were rare so early in the winter in Lakeport. This one couldn't have come at a better time so far as the children were concerned. Not only had all the schools been forced to close, but some of the snow was bound to be around so they could have a white Christmas.

Flossie clapped her hands excitedly as she watched the coal-black mare standing near the curb. The horse was pawing the snow and tossing her head impatiently.

"Something's bothering her," the little girl said.

Out of nowhere a snowball whizzed through the air and hit the animal on the side of the head. She whinnied and, with a jerk, started off down the street.

"She's running away!" Flossie shrieked.

Chasing the horse as fast as they could, the twins yelled, "Whoa! Whoa!"

The animal paid no attention. Other children who were playing in the snow also cried out, but it was no use.

Covering her eyes with her chubby fingers, Flossie gasped. "If she doesn't stop, she'll hit somebody!"

As she spoke, three figures hidden beneath layers of clothing appeared in the distance. "There's Bert and Nan with Charlie Mason!" Freddie exclaimed. Bert and Nan were Freddie and Flossie's brother and sister, the dark-haired twelve-year-old Bobbsey twins. Charlie Mason was Bert's best friend.

Seeing the horse, Bert and Charlie darted after it, waving their arms frantically.

"Be careful!" Flossie shouted. The animal zigzagged in front of them.

Bert and Charlie separated, running next to the horse on either side. Each boy grabbed the bridle strap near the horse's mouth.

"Whoa!" Bert commanded with a forceful tug.

At last, the mare slowed to a stop and Bert jumped into the sleigh.

"Here, Bert," Charlie said, throwing him the reins.

"You were fantastic!" Nan Bobbsey said to the boys. The slim, attractive girl had rushed forward and begun stroking the horse's head.

As the animal grew quiet, the white-haired driver emerged from a backyard to find his horse and sleigh gone. "What happened?" he asked, hurrying down the street.

Everyone began talking at once.

"I gather you're the one who stopped Daisy," the elderly man said to Bert.

"Charlie and I both did, sir" was the answer.

"I've seen you around Lakeport before. Your name is—" His pale blue eyes stared intently at the boy.

"Bert Bobbsey," the boy said.

"Richard Bobbsey's son?"

The boy nodded proudly and introduced Nan and the smaller twins.

"Well, thanks again," he said, walking toward the sleigh. "You know, five years ago a Bobbsey tried to help me out. Today the Bobbseys did me a second favor. Strange, isn't it? Wonder if this'll be the last time, or—"

"Excuse me, sir?" Bert said.

"Nothing!" came the blunt return.

Bert flushed. "I-I don't understand. You said it has been five years—"

A sad, thoughtful look spread across the seamed face.

"Forget I said that," the man barked.

His sudden gruffness not only disturbed the Bobbseys, but it also made them curious.

Bert wondered why the man was driving an old-fashioned sleigh. It must be a lot of fun, the boy thought, but the owner looked so unhappy.

Suddenly Freddie blurted out, "You sure are a mysterious Santa Claus!"

"Yes, my friend," said the man. "And my mystery is my own business."

Seeing how serious everyone looked, the man brightened and chuckled. Then he pulled a wad of money from his pocket and gave it to Bert.

Seeing how much there was, Bert gulped. "I can't accept this, sir," he insisted.

"Don't be shy, son. Go ahead. Take it. I want you and your friends to have a real nice Christmas treat on me."

The crisp new bills crackled in Bert's palm. "Wow! Thanks, Mr. . . . uh—?"

There was no answer as the mysterious driver boarded his sleigh, gave the reins a hard shake, and sped away. Either he had not heard the question or—and this seemed more likely to Bert, though he couldn't say why—he did not wish to reveal his name.

"Wait a minute." Bert's palm flew to his forehead. "He must be the man who delivers gifts all over town at Christmas."

"To all the disadvantaged families—that's right!" Nan said, watching the sleigh drift out of sight. "I was wondering if we'd ever meet him. This year, because of the snow, he even got to do it in a sleigh."

"So he is a kind of Santa Claus," Flossie added.

"I wonder what he was doing *here*," said Bert. "Our neighbors aren't exactly disadvantaged."

"Maybe he knows something we don't know," said Nan.

As they stood and puzzled over the situation, a young woman who was standing nearby and had witnessed the black horse's rescue said, "Excuse me, but I know that man's name. It's Jess Carford. He owns Snow Lodge at the other end of Lake Metoka."

"He looks so miserable," Freddie commented.

Creasing her lips into a thin line, the woman replied, "The last thing I heard, Mr. Carford doesn't live there anymore. I also heard it has to do with some mystery at the lodge. What mystery I don't know. You'd have to ask him."

So there really was a mystery! The twins raced home, hoping their mother could tell them about it. Mr. Bobbsey had left on a business trip just before the snow. He owned a large lumberyard located on the shore of Lake Metoka and frequently went out of town to purchase supplies.

"Daddy'll be home for Christmas, won't he?" Flossie inquired after she had taken off her coat and boots.

"Of course he will, dear," said her pretty dark-haired mother. "He'll be back in a couple of days."

Bert told his mother about meeting Mr. Carford. "We were wondering what you knew about the mystery at Snow Lodge," he said.

Mrs. Bobbsey lowered her gaze. "As I recall, it had to do with Mr. Carford's family."

"He acted a little grumpy when we tried to talk to him," Nan said.

Her mother nodded as if she wasn't surprised. "Perhaps he doesn't want to discuss it," Mrs. Bobbsey added gravely. "If you see him again, I think it would be best not to bring up the subject. Agreed?"

"A-greed," Freddie and Flossie chimed in halfheartedly. Their mother's soft brown eyes shifted to Bert and Nan.

"Whatever you say, Mom," Bert replied.

"Good."

The twin detectives were not happy. How could they solve the mystery at Snow Lodge if they couldn't ask Mr. Carford about it?

■ 2 ■
The Snow Battle

Disappointed, the young detectives said no more about the mystery.

"That's that, I guess," Bert said, frowning.

"Guess so," Nan echoed under her breath. "We'll just have to find something else to do."

The next day Bert and three of his friends, including Charlie Mason, decided to build a snow fort. They chose a vacant lot near the Bobbsey lumberyard.

"Don't let the sunshine fool you now. It's still cold outside," Dinah said, handing Bert his woolen cap. Dinah was the Bobbseys' housekeeper, an attractive black woman with warm sable eyes.

"Thanks," Bert replied, though he was clearly more interested in the small silvery plastic bag she was holding. "What's in there?"

"Doughnuts, as if you didn't know. I baked

10

them fresh this morning in case you get hungry later."

Dinah Johnson and her husband, Sam, lived in a cozy cottage behind the Bobbseys' house. Sam was the foreman at Mr. Bobbsey's lumberyard. The family was very fond of both of the Johnsons.

"You know what?" Bert said, taking the bag and sprinting down the steps.

"No, what?" Dinah asked.

"You're better than a bucket of ice cream!"

The woman smiled, watching the boy disappear up the street. "Keep that hat on, you hear me?" she called after him.

The winter sunshine had started to melt the snow around town. But it wasn't as successful on the deeper snow out by the lake. Bert and the other boys set to work on the fort immediately. They were just finishing when the school bully, Danny Rugg, and several of his friends came by.

"I'm taking over now," Danny insisted, ordering them away.

"Who says?" Bert asked.

"I say."

"We built this fort and we're staying right here," Charlie Mason declared.

That was all Danny needed to hear. The snowball fight was on! His companions took cover behind nearby trees and began pounding the fort with snowballs.

Bert motioned to his friends to duck below the walls. Soon the boys had their own stockpile of snowballs. They waited for Danny's next move.

Gloating, he stepped from behind the tree. "Come on, everybody, let's capture the fort from those creeps!" he commanded.

At the last minute, as the bully's gang drew nearer, Bert yelled, *"Fire!"*

A hail of snowballs descended instantly on the startled attackers. They staggered back with their arms in front of them to ward off the snowballs.

Danny gave another frantic order, and the group retreated hastily. They huddled together just out of firing range.

"He's up to some trick," Bert warned, packing a snowball.

Several tense moments passed. More snowballs were made and snow was packed against the thick four-foot-high walls of the fort.

Suddenly Danny waved a white handkerchief tied to a broken branch. He walked slowly toward the fort. His gang spread out in a semicircle behind him.

"They're surrendering!" Charlie Mason exclaimed, leaping to his feet. "We've won!"

In that instant, a shower of snowballs filled the air. *Splat!* One struck Charlie squarely in the chest, knocking him to the ground.

"Down! Everybody down!" Bert shouted. He crawled over to his injured friend. "Charlie, are you okay?"

"I'm fine. The wind just got knocked out of me for a second."

Bert examined the hard icy snowball that had hit the boy. "There's a stone in the center of this!"

"No wonder it hurt so much," Charlie remarked, rubbing the sore spot.

"It's time to teach those guys a lesson!" Bert said. His fist crushed the snow.

As quickly as they could, the group stuffed snowballs inside their jackets and pockets. Bert took the lead. He burst out of the fort toward the trees where Danny and the rest had vanished after the sneak attack. Bert and his friends pelted them with snowballs from every direction.

"Stop!" the bully pleaded. Spattered from head to foot, he limped into view as his army fled in confusion. "I'll get you for this, Bert Bobbsey," Danny said in a threatening voice.

"We beat you fairly—and we didn't use stones!" Charlie said. "Go home, Danny."

Fuming, the mean boy stomped across the lot.

"How many for hot chocolate and homemade doughnuts?" Bert asked, offering his bag of doughnuts to his companions. "The hot chocolate's on Mr. Carford."

Whooping for joy, the boys munched on doughnuts all the way to the center of town, where they went inside Jenkins's Soda Shop. They took seats at the counter while Bert placed the order. In a moment four large frothy cups appeared, filled with the rich-flavored chocolate and a mountain of homemade whipped cream.

When the last delicious drops were finally gone, Bert glanced over at the clock on the wall. "It's almost five. We'd better go home," he said.

Outside, the boys said good-bye and scattered in different directions. The sky had grown dark, and a few soft white flakes had begun to fall. Bert walked rapidly. He removed his wet gloves, blew on his icy fingers, and dug into the shrunken bag. There was one doughnut left, which he devoured as he crossed Main Street.

"Eight more blocks," the boy thought, throwing the bag into a corner litter basket as a car pulled up.

"Want a lift?" a familiar voice called. "It's awfully cold out tonight."

Bert peered into the car at the white hair and lined face of Mr. Carford. Bert hesitated. Although he knew of the man's kindly reputation,

Mr. Carford was still a stranger. He thought a minute, decided he would be safe, and accepted the offer.

But as Bert took a step, his foot slipped on the frozen curb and he plunged facedown onto the car seat.

"Easy, son. Not hurt, are you?" the man inquired.

"I'm all right." Bert patted the seat and felt around the floor mat. "I thought I heard something fall out of my pocket. Guess not, though."

"It wasn't your wallet, was it?"

"No, it's right here."

"Well, if I do find anything, I'll give you a call," Mr. Carford said, pressing on the accelerator. "You know, it isn't often that Daisy runs away as she did yesterday."

Bert was tempted to ask his new friend about the mystery at Snow Lodge. But he remembered his mother's advice and said nothing. In a little while the car swung to a stop in front of the Bobbsey house and the boy said good-bye.

Freddie and Flossie met him at the door. They were dressed in snowsuits, hats, scarves, and mittens.

"Going sledding in the dark?" Bert asked, giving his brother a playful poke.

"We're trying to keep warm," Freddie said. "It's freezing in here."

"What happened?"

"Mommy says there's something wrong with the furnace. The heat keeps going up and down."

Mrs. Bobbsey explained that repairmen were in the basement trying to fix it.

Shortly one of them came upstairs and stripped off his work gloves. "We did our best," he said, "but I can't promise how long it'll last. You really need a new unit."

Thinking about the upcoming holidays, Mrs. Bobbsey said, "This couldn't have happened at a worse time. Is there any chance of getting a new furnace this week?"

"Before Christmas?" the repairman said. "We can start, but we couldn't finish the job until afterward. If you want us to begin work tomorrow, you ought to plan to go someplace else for Christmas."

Mrs. Bobbsey said she would have to consult her husband and contact the service office later.

In a few minutes, however, the house was fairly comfortable again. The children took off their coats and settled down to an excited discussion of where they would stay while the furnace was being repaired.

"We could go to Africa," Freddie proposed.

"That's a little far. What about Florida?" Nan said.

"Hold on, you two," Mrs. Bobbsey spoke. "Who said we're going anywhere? We'll probably have heat for quite a while yet."

"But what if we don't? What if the furnace stops completely all of a sudden, and we start turning into human icicles?" Nan asked. "And what about when the men take out this furnace, before they can put in the new one?"

"I suppose we'll have to move to the Lakeport Hotel. Don't worry. Your father and I will figure something out."

Next morning, Lakeport was a sparkling white fairyland.

Flossie pranced in front of her bedroom window. "Oh, the whole world's covered with vanilla frosting!" she giggled.

Another feathery layer of snow softened the outlines of trees and houses, and the streets were hidden under a silent white blanket. But the new snow wasn't deep, and school was open.

After breakfast, both sets of twins put on their warmest clothing, said good-bye to their two pets—Snap, a big shaggy white dog, and Snoop, their black cat—and left for school.

When they arrived, they were amazed to see a large crowd of children gathered at the entrance and ran to join them. In front of the door was an enormous frozen snowball that the janitor was struggling to move.

"Let me help," Bert offered, squeezing forward. Together with several other boys, he heaved his weight against the huge mass while the man used a long metal rod as a lever to pry it loose.

"Whoever did this soaked it with water, and now it's frozen solid to the step," the janitor said.

Just then a teacher appeared and directed the children to a side entrance.

"You go on in, too," the janitor told Bert.

"Are you sure you don't want us to stick around?" the boy asked.

"No, no. This snowball will be gone in no time," the janitor said. He rocked the lever again as Bert and the others went to their homerooms.

Later that morning a special assembly was called in the auditorium, and the children filed quietly through the corridors.

Shaking his head, Bert whispered to Nan, "I'll bet this assembly is because of the snowball. And if it is, somebody's going to be in plenty of trouble!"

∎ 3 ∎

Initial Evidence

When everyone was seated, Mr. Tetlow, the tall gray-haired principal, mounted the stage to speak. From the look on his face, it was obvious Bert was right.

"It's against the fire laws to block the entrance to a school building," the principal stated. "However, if the students who put the snowball there come forward now, I promise you there will be no punishment."

He paused and waited. The auditorium was very quiet. No one moved.

"Well," Mr. Tetlow continued, "I have to tell you I have evidence that definitely identifies one of the troublemakers." Still no one stood up. "I'll be in my office all day if anyone wants to see me. Assembly dismissed!"

"Whoever did it ought to admit it," Charlie said to Bert. "Mr. Tetlow says he has evidence."

Bert agreed. But by lunchtime no one had

confessed, and there were all sorts of rumors about who the mysterious culprit was.

Toward the end of the day, a student came into Bert's homeroom with a message from the principal's office. Startled, Nan looked up as her twin shut his desk abruptly and left the room.

What does Mr. Tetlow want me for? Bert thought. I hope he doesn't think I put that snowball on the front step.

However, as the boy detective stood in front of the principal's desk, Mr. Tetlow rubbed his chin thoughtfully and gazed out the window.

"I'm very disappointed in you, Bert. I've waited all day for you to come in." Bert gulped. "I'll give you one more chance. Is there something you want to tell me?"

"A-about the snowball, you mean? No, sir. I had nothing to do with it!"

Reaching for something in his desk drawer, the principal said, "This penknife was found by the janitor *under* the snowball. It has your initials on the handle. Does it belong to you?" Mr. Tetlow displayed the silvery object.

Without examining the knife, Bert recognized it instantly. "Yes—yes, sir, it does."

An uncomfortable silence followed. "Mr. Tetlow," said Bert, "I think I can prove my innocence, if you let me."

The principal nodded.

21

"May I use your telephone, sir?" the boy asked.

"You may."

Quickly Bert looked up Mr. Carford's phone number in the local directory and placed the call.

"Hello, Mr. Carford?" the boy said. "It's Bert Bobbsey." There was a long pause as the elderly man sneezed and chatted about the weather. "I'm sorry you have a cold, Mr. Carford, but—"

The boy pressed his cheek to the receiver as the conversation droned on. Then suddenly Bert's dour expression changed. "You did? Wow! That's great! Would you mind telling this to my school principal?" He handed the phone to Mr. Tetlow, who listened intently.

Afterward, Bert explained, "I was walking home, when Mr. Carford drove by in his car and offered me a ride. I started to get in the front seat and stumbled. That's when my knife must've fallen out of my pocket."

"According to Mr. Carford," Mr. Tetlow said, "Jimmy Belton stopped by his house with a delivery from his father's pharmacy for Mr. Carford's sister. Jimmy said he was going right back into town."

"So naturally Mr. Carford gave Jimmy the knife to return to me," Bert deduced.

Buzzing his secretary, Mr. Tetlow asked her to

bring Jimmy Belton to his office at once. A good-natured spindly boy, well-liked by everyone, he appeared in the doorway, nervously biting his lower lip.

"After Mr. Carford gave you Bert's knife, what did you do with it?" the principal questioned.

"I gave it to Danny Rugg," Jimmy admitted. "I met him on the way to the Bobbseys. He asked me why I was going there, and I told him. He said he'd return the knife for me."

"Let's get Danny in here right away," Mr. Tetlow said grimly.

In a minute the bully swaggered into the principal's office with a look of bravado on his face. But when he saw Bert, Jimmy, and the principal glance from him to the penknife, the look vanished.

"Danny, I want the truth now. Did you put Bert's knife under that snowball?" Mr. Tetlow asked sternly.

The bully hung his head and managed to choke out, "Y-yes."

"You owe Bert an apology," the man said.

Danny's eyes blazed with fury.

"We're waiting," Mr. Tetlow continued.

Still resistant, Danny lowered his head and mumbled, "I apologize."

"Okay, Danny," Bert said generously.

Mr. Tetlow rose from his chair. "Now, Danny, I'm quite sure you didn't put that snowball on the steps all by yourself. When you tell your friends you've confessed, they will want to do the same. Ask them to come to my office immediately."

As he finished speaking, his secretary's voice interrupted over the intercom. "Mr. Tetlow, there's someone here to see you. A Mr. Carford," she said.

"Oh, by all means, send him in."

As Mr. Carford stepped through the door he sneezed into a large white handkerchief, then stuffed it into his pocket. "I don't want to give anybody my cold, so I won't shake your hand, Mr. Tetlow," he said, smiling pleasantly. "After I hung up the phone, I got to thinking. I figured you wouldn't have called me unless Bert was in serious trouble. He's a good boy, you know. He helped me out the other day."

Mr. Tetlow explained the details of what had happened earlier that morning and how suspicion had fallen on the boy.

"Well, I'm here to vouch for him," Mr. Carford said. "He's not the sort of kid who would do what you described."

"I realize that," Mr. Tetlow agreed. "Rest assured, everything has been straightened out. It was very nice of you to come over. Bert and I both appreciate it."

Mr. Carford blew into his handkerchief again. "Anytime."

A step ahead of Bert, the elderly man left the room first.

"Thanks a lot for coming over," the boy said, escorting his friend to the door of the building.

"I'm always glad to do a favor for a Bobbsey. You rescued Daisy for me! Besides—"

Bert waited to hear more, but Mr. Carford caught himself and strode quickly toward his car.

What else had he wanted to say? Bert wondered, his curiosity growing. Maybe it had something to do with Snow Lodge!

I can't figure him out, the young detective mused. One minute he's so nice and friendly, and the next minute, he closes up like a clam shell.

When school was over, Bert and Charlie headed past the principal's office as a group of boys were walking inside. "That's Danny's gang," Charlie observed. "Danny sure went to an awful lot of trouble to get even with you. I hope he gets a million detentions."

"If he gets half a million, I'll be happy." Bert chuckled. "Let's go."

When Bert was a few blocks from home, Nan caught up to him. "Tell me what happened. What did Mr. Tetlow say?" she asked.

Bert told her about the phone call. Then he added, "I didn't expect Mr. Carford to show up. He was great. He said he was always glad to do a favor for a Bobbsey. But then the strangest thing happened. He started to say more, and stopped. I'm positive it was about the mystery."

"The minute Dad comes home we have to ask him what this is about. Maybe we can help Mr. Carford."

By this time the children, including the younger twins, had reached the Bobbsey house, and their mother met them at the door. Bert told everyone about the huge snowball and Mr. Carford's help.

"Why are you wearing your heavy sweater, Mommy?" Flossie asked. "Did the furnace stop?"

"No, dear. I just don't want to run it too much. You'd all better put on extra sweaters." Mrs. Bobbsey sighed anxiously. "I called every hotel in the area, and they're all booked solid."

"Why don't we stay with Dinah and Sam?" Freddie said.

"Come to think of it, they are planning to visit relatives over Christmas. But their place really is too small for all of us," Mrs. Bobbsey said. "Oh,

I almost forgot. There are two letters on the mantel, one for Bert and one for Nan."

"Hooray!" Bert exclaimed. "Mine's from Hal." Hal was Harry Bobbsey, the son of the twins' Uncle Daniel, who lived at Meadowbrook Farm. "Listen to this:

> '*Just between you and me, Bert, I'm going to have a terrible Christmas. Mom and Dad and I are going to visit Aunt Martha. She must be at least a hundred, and there isn't anyone to play with. I'll be so glad when we get home again!*'"

"Who's *your* letter from?" Bert asked Nan.

"Dot. She's really upset."

Their cousin, Dorothy Minturn, lived in Ocean Cliff with her parents. Her mother was Mrs. Bobbsey's sister.

"Uncle William and Aunt Emily are taking her to Florida over Christmas vacation," Nan said, "but Dot would rather be where there's snow."

"What a shame," Mrs. Bobbsey remarked.

"Wouldn't it be great if we could all spend Christmas together?" Bert piped up.

"It would be a cousin Christmas," Flossie said. "Wait till we tell Daddy."

"Not so fast," said Mrs. Bobbsey. "We haven't even found a place to stay."

After school the next day, the twins decided to go to the lumberyard office to see if Mr. Bobbsey had returned.

"Oh, Daddy, Daddy!" Flossie cried, springing into her father's arms.

Everyone talked at once. It was several minutes before Bert had a chance to mention the mysterious Mr. Carford.

"Dad, what did he mean about a Bobbsey coming into his life five years ago?"

"Well, Bert—"

Relieved by the jingling telephone, Mr. Bobbsey grabbed the receiver. "Excuse me, will you?" he said to the caller, and he told the children he had an important long-distance call. "You'd better go home now. I'll see you all at supper."

Discouraged, the four detectives waved goodbye and left. Again, they would have to wait for their father's answer.

"I have a hunch Dad doesn't want to talk about Mr. Carford," Nan said. "And if he doesn't, we may never find out any more about him."

▪ 4 ▪
Sad Story

Halfway home, the Bobbseys heard the sudden tinkling sound of bells behind them. Turning, they saw Mr. Carford's beautiful old sleigh gliding up the street.

Sunlight glinted off the runners as he drew up next to the twins. Daisy whinnied.

"How are you feeling?" Bert inquired.

"Just fine, thank you," answered Mr. Carford, blowing his cherry-red nose. "How would you children like to have a sleigh ride out to my house? My sister baked some Christmas cookies this morning. I snitched one, and my goodness, it was"— he kissed his fingertips —"out of this world!"

Freddie and Flossie giggled.

"We'd love to come," Nan said.

"Wonderful. First, let's be sure it's all right with your mother."

After obtaining permission from Mrs. Bobbsey, the older children climbed excitedly into the rear seat of the sleigh while the younger ones took seats on either side of Mr. Carford.

"Okay, Daisy, let's go," he said, giving a gentle slap of the reins.

The sled headed for the old farmhouse. Nestled among tall majestic pines, it had a shingled roof and a huge gray-stone chimney through which smoke curled gently into the crisp afternoon air. The children scrambled to the ground as a plump woman with short ringlets of silver hair came to the front door.

"This is my sister, Emma Carford," said their host.

"How do you do and welcome," she said cheerily. "Now come inside. I have everything all set up in the dining room." She took their coats while Mr. Carford put Daisy in the stall.

On the table was a pretty white tablecloth with dainty embroidered holly leaves, red-and-green napkins, a big platter of cookies, and a pitcher of milk.

"Yummy!" Flossie said, sampling one of the cookies.

"You're a great cook!" exclaimed Freddie, who considered himself an expert on such matters. The others laughed.

"Thank you, Freddie. That's a real compliment," Emma Carford said, noticing the empty platter. "If you're done, we want to take you all on a tour of the house."

Nan loved the old-fashioned four-poster beds on the second floor. They were covered with white ruffled canopies and homemade patchwork quilts.

Mr. Carford showed Bert his collection of Toby mugs, which he had obtained in England. Many of the little containers, all of them shaped like jolly stout figures in three-cornered hats, had been made before the Revolutionary War.

"Do you have any plans for Christmas vacation?" Mr. Carford asked.

"We're probably going to have a hotel Christmas," Freddie replied mournfully.

"A what?"

Nan and Bert told Mr. Carford about the problem with the furnace.

The Carfords made no comment but led the group to the kitchen, where there was a wide fireplace with a raised hearth.

"I copied this fireplace from one in Snow Lodge. How my brothers and sisters and I loved to sit by that one when we were children! It was a grand way to spend a long winter evening after a hard day's work on the farm, if you know what I mean."

Snow Lodge! Perhaps the twins would finally learn something about the mystery!

"Our parents died when we were small," Mr. Carford said. "Snow Lodge had to be sold, and each of us went to live with a different older relative. Over the years all except Emma and myself were married, and we gradually lost touch with the rest."

The man stared into the crackling fire. "After I grew up, I went to New York, where I had quite a good business for a long time. Then I retired and returned to Lakeport. That's when I bought back Snow Lodge. Strange as it may sound, I was hoping members of my family would come to live with me at the lodge. But it was too late. They all had their own homes."

"What a shame," Nan said.

"Now, don't you go feeling sorry for me. I've been happy most of my life. Remodeling Snow Lodge was a pleasure for me. When it was done, I got word that my sister Louise's husband died, leaving her with a ten-year-old boy, Dave, and very little money. They turned to me, of course.

"However, not long after they arrived in Lakeport, Louise became ill," Mr. Carford said. "She passed away, so I brought Dave up alone. He was like a son to me. We did everything together. We took hikes. We fished. We hunted."

A pained expression flickered briefly on the man's face. "About five years ago, we had a misunderstanding, and Dave left Snow Lodge. He said he'd never come back unless— There I go again, dwelling on things that can't be changed.

"I closed Snow Lodge and hired a neighboring farmer to look after it. When Emma here wrote that she wanted to stay with me, I bought this farmhouse."

As if to punctuate the end of his story, he slapped his knee. "You'll have to forgive an old man for talking so long," he said. "I'd better take you home now."

"We had a lovely time," Nan said after each of the children had thanked Emma Carford.

When they reached the Bobbsey house, Nan invited Mr. Carford to come in.

"As a matter of fact, I was just about to invite myself," the man replied.

Greeting their guest cordially, the twins' father introduced him to Mrs. Bobbsey.

"I hear you're having furnace trouble," Mr. Carford said casually, drawing a key case from his pocket. "These belong to Snow Lodge. I'd be very happy if you and your family would spend the holidays there."

"That's very generous of you," Mrs. Bobbsey said, "but—"

"No buts about it. I insist. There's plenty to do up there," Mr. Carford said. "Ice skating, skiing, sledding. And if you children want to play indoors, there are trunks in the attic with lots of

old-fashioned clothing in them, not to mention all kinds of secret closets. I don't know anyone who'd enjoy the place more except—"

Faltering, he looked briefly at Mr. Bobbsey.

"Would you mind, Mr. Carford, if we brought our two cousins with us?" Bert asked. "Is it okay, Mom, Dad?"

"So long as Mr. Carford doesn't mind," Mrs. Bobbsey said.

"The more the merrier, I always say." The elderly man brightened again.

After all the calls and arrangements had been made for Harry and Dorothy to come, Bert found his longed-for opportunity. He asked his father about the mystery at Snow Lodge.

"Dad, did you ever do a favor for Mr. Carford? He told us how he brought up his nephew. I wondered if it had something to do with that."

Mr. Bobbsey drew in his breath. "It's not a very happy tale, son, and frankly, I was hoping you wouldn't ask me again," he said. "Mr. Carford gave the boy everything. Dave liked spending money on his own, too. Although his uncle gave him a generous allowance, the boy wanted more. After he turned eighteen, he asked Mr. Carford for a large sum of money. His uncle refused.

"They had an argument. Later on, Mr. Carford discovered a stack of bills missing from the mantelpiece where he had left them. He had sold one of his horses that morning, and he was intending to put the money in the bank that afternoon." Mr. Bobbsey paused. "Dave was the only other person home."

"So Mr. Carford accused him of stealing the money?" Bert finished.

"Dave denied it, but his uncle didn't believe him. They had a bitter quarrel, and Dave left Snow Lodge. Naturally, he was hurt. He vowed never to return or to see Mr. Carford again until his name was cleared of all wrongdoing."

"What a pity!" Mrs. Bobbsey sighed. "But you did help him, Dick."

"I tried, anyway. Personally, I never doubted that Dave was innocent. He may have been foolish at times, but he wasn't dishonest," Mr. Bobbsey went on. "I found him a room in town and gave him a job at the lumberyard until he could decide what else to do. That was five years ago."

"What does Dave do now?" Bert inquired.

"In the winter he guides sportsmen through the woods. He has a little cabin not far from Snow Lodge. When summer rolls around, he heads north to help the fishermen."

"What became of the money?" Nan asked.

"That's still a mystery," Mr. Bobbsey replied. "For a while Mr. Carford thought a prowler had

36

broken in, but the police found no evidence. Finally, they determined that the money had fallen into the fireplace, where logs were burning, and was destroyed."

"No wonder Mr. Carford gets so upset when he talks about it," Nan said. "He must really miss his nephew."

"You know, aside from Mr. Carford's sister, Emma, Dave is his only heir. I think the old gentleman would give anything to forget the incident, but Dave is very proud."

"When we get to Snow Lodge, let's hunt for the money," Freddie said.

"Oh, yes," Flossie agreed, "right away!"

■ 5 ■
Tricks

School ended promptly at noon the next day, marking the beginning of the Christmas vacation. The Bobbseys hurried home and found Dinah putting a large fruitcake in a holiday tin.

"The packing's almost done," Dinah told the children. "Your mother's working on the last suitcase now."

"Isn't it exciting?" Flossie said. "When will Dot and Hal be here?"

"Later this afternoon," Nan replied.

Wiping her forehead, Dinah glanced at the kitchen clock. "I'm running a little late today," she muttered. "Soup and sandwiches coming right up."

"May I have a candy?" Freddie asked, eyeing a bag of foil-wrapped chocolate.

"No, you may not," Dinah said. "Those are for Snow Lodge."

The little boy giggled. "Snow Lodge doesn't eat candy."

"You know what I mean." The housekeeper smiled.

When the children had finished their lunch, they heard the front doorbell ring. "I'll get it," Flossie said, skipping into the hall.

To her delight, it was Mr. Carford. "Who can help me deliver presents today?" he asked.

"I can," Flossie answered immediately.

"So can I," her twin added, dashing to get his coat.

Nan and Bert, meanwhile, had promised to go skating with their friends and waved as the other children rushed to the sleigh.

Flossie noticed a toy hook-and-ladder sticking out of her brother's jacket. "What's that?" she inquired.

Freddie blushed. "An extra gift," he said. Then he pointed to the small doll in Flossie's hand. "What's that?"

"An extra gift," she remarked, "in case Santa needs it."

On the way to the first house, Mr. Carford said he was delighted the Bobbseys were going to Snow Lodge. "Your mother says you're going up there tomorrow."

"And we're going to look and look—"

A sharp elbow jab in the ribs by Flossie made Freddie hiccup. It was her way of warning him not to give away their search plan for the missing money. Bringing up the subject would remind Mr. Carford of his nephew and the awful thing that had happened.

"You're going to look—?" the man prompted.

"Oh, yes!" Freddie managed to say. "All around your wonderful house. We can't wait!"

Flossie winked at her twin. He had managed to change the subject.

After Mr. Carford left an unusually large box of toys at a shabby-looking house on the far side of town, he climbed into the sleigh once again.

"Are you sick?" Flossie asked, observing his doleful expression.

"Oh, no, I'm practically over my cold," he said. "I was just thinking of how much that place reminds me of the one I lived in with my aunt and uncle after my parents died. They were very poor, too."

"What was it like when you were little like me?" Flossie urged, sliding her hand into Mr. Carford's large warm palm.

Flicking the reins with his other hand, he said, "There's not much to tell. But one thing I do remember—at Christmas when I was ten years old, I saw a kite in a toy-store window. It was the

40

most beautiful one I'd ever seen—red and yellow with a long skinny tail. I wanted it so badly, but I never said a word about it. I knew my uncle couldn't afford to buy it."

"Is that why you give so many toys away now?" asked Flossie.

"Yes, but I like doing it, too," he said. "Giddap, Daisy!"

"We brought some presents, too," Freddie announced. He showed his toy hook–and–ladder while Flossie proudly displayed her doll.

"Thank you, Santa Freddie. Thank you, Santa Flossie," Mr. Carford said. "I know a boy and girl who'll be very happy to get these."

At each of the homes Mr. Carford visited, he spoke to the children's parents and suggested they save their gifts for Christmas morning. Finally the back of the sleigh was completely empty.

"Looks like we're done," Mr. Carford said. The sleigh bells jingled spiritedly as he started to sing "Jolly Old St. Nicholas," and the twins joined in the chorus.

Soon after they were home again, Nan and Bert arrived with their father and Harry. There was an enthusiastic welcome for the tall farm boy who, winter and summer, had a deep ruddy tan.

"Where's Dot?" Flossie asked.

"Here I am!" the dark-haired girl called through the front door. She plopped a big shopping bag on the floor. "Mom and Dad send their love and a bunch of Christmas goodies. They're in this bag. That's why it's so fat." She laughed.

"Played any tricks lately?" Mrs. Bobbsey asked. Dorothy was known for playing practical jokes.

"Not yet," she said, chuckling.

Bert jingled the coins in his pants pocket. "Wouldn't it be great if we could find Mr. Carford's missing money?"

Quickly Nan told her cousins about the trouble between Mr. Carford and his nephew.

"But let's not find the money right away," Flossie said, changing her mind, "'cause if we do, we might have to move out of Snow Lodge so they could move back in."

Mr. Bobbsey smiled. "Honey, if the police couldn't find the money—not even a clue to it—you don't have to worry about *when* you'll find it. The real question is *if!*"

His daughter nodded sheepishly. "I have to put my doll's nightgown in her suitcase," she announced importantly.

Freddie also wandered off to his room. A minute later he let out a loud yell, pounded down the stairs, and lurched into the living room wild-eyed.

"It's in my room! A-a big bear. He growled at me, and his eyes—they're real big and mean!"

"A bear!" Harry exclaimed. "How did a bear get into the house?"

"I don't know," Freddie answered.

Wasting no time, Mr. Bobbsey and Bert soared up the stairs with Nan at their heels. In a corner of Freddie's room were two glaring beady eyes.

"Oh!" Nan exclaimed.

Instantly Mr. Bobbsey switched on the light. There was a bear in the room all right—a toy bear with battery-lighted eyes. Seated next to it was Dorothy, making the scariest noises.

"You scared me!" Freddie shouted, peering at her.

"And here I lugged this nice bear all the way from home just for you," the girl said, pretending to be hurt. "I guess you don't want it."

Freddie beamed. "But I do—"

As he spoke, the telephone rang and Bert sprang to the hall to answer it. "Yes, we're leaving tomorrow morning. We'll be there about a week. No problem. Good-bye."

"Who was it, Bert?" Mr. Bobbsey asked, looking over the banister.

"Some man from the *Lakeport News*. He writes the social column. He wants to put a line in his column about our trip."

Mrs. Bobbsey looked troubled as she and her husband hastened downstairs with the other children. "The social page is run by Clara Estes. I know her well, and she doesn't have a male assistant."

"Should we tell the police?" Bert asked.

"Definitely," his father replied, going to the phone. "He could be a burglar."

To everyone's relief, the police captain promised to keep an eye on the house while the family was away.

"Mom, I'm really sorry I talked to that guy," Bert said.

"Don't worry about it. Next time you'll be more careful."

To everyone's surprise, the knocker on the front door now began rapping loudly. "I'll get it," Bert said. "Maybe it's the police."

However, no one was there.

"Bert? Is something wrong?" his father asked as everyone gathered in the living room.

Bert was fumbling with a sheet of paper that he had just removed from an envelope. "This was under the door," he said. "I looked outside, but no one was there."

"What does it say?" Mrs. Bobbsey asked.

There was a puzzled, almost frightened expression on Bert's face as he spoke. "It's addressed to the Bobbsey twins. It says:

> '*Stay away from Snow Lodge! If you don't, you'll be sorry. The Green Monster will get you all!*' "

"Green Monster!" Freddie repeated as Bert handed the message to his father. The little boy's body shook.

Flossie clung to her mother while Mr. Bobbsey examined the coarse white paper.

"There's nothing to be afraid of," he said. "There's no such thing as a 'Green Monster.' One of your friends must be playing a joke on you."

All eyes turned on Dorothy. "You know I haven't been out of this room," she said, defending herself.

"I'm positive it was Danny," Bert insisted. "In fact, I can prove that Danny wrote this silly thing. Someone in class passed around a sheet of paper the other day, and we all wrote poems on it. It was sort of a holiday greeting to our teachers. Remember, Nan?"

"Yes, I do. I brought the poems home and

copied them in green ink on a piece of red Christmas paper," his twin added. "The original is still on my desk. I'll get it."

Nan returned with the sheet of notebook paper on which there were a number of handwritten verses. The older twins scanned them rapidly until they came to one signed by Danny Rugg.

"Here it is," Bert said.

Sensing that something was wrong, Mrs. Bobbsey said, "Well, while you're reading poetry, Freddie and Flossie have to get ready for bed." She scooped up the younger children and whisked them away.

"Dad, this note wasn't written by Danny at all," Bert confided under his breath. "It looks like a man's handwriting."

"Which means there's more to this mystery than any of us realized," Nan said.

▪ 6 ▪

A Spooky Tour

As Nan stared at the mysterious message, she asked, "Could Dave Burdock, Mr. Carford's nephew, have written this?"

"Not a chance," Mr. Bobbsey replied. "Dave's too decent a guy. Besides, how would he know we were going there?"

Harry crouched over and doubled up his fists. "Okay, Green Monster, come and get it, and see how long you last!"

"No matter who wrote that note," Mrs. Bobbsey said, "I don't want anyone to worry about it. Obviously it's someone's warped idea of a joke."

"And we're not going to let it ruin our fun," Dorothy added.

The next morning everyone was up early. Nan helped her mother put last-minute items in suitcases while Dorothy assisted Flossie in wrapping Christmas packages. There were many secret conferences between the girls and much giggling and rustling of paper and ribbon.

One of Mr. Bobbsey's employees from the lumberyard stopped by to pick up Snoop. The crew was going to look after him while the family was gone. Snap, on the other hand, was going along to Snow Lodge.

Next the boys helped Mr. Bobbsey pack the van. Soon all of the bags were stowed in the back of the vehicle, and the engine was humming low.

"Just think," Mr. Bobbsey said as the children piled inside, "when we all get back, we'll have a nice new furnace to keep us warm."

"Good-bye, house," Freddie said.

"Good-bye, door. Good-bye, window." Flossie chuckled.

But in a while the conversation turned to the Green Monster and the mystery of Snow Lodge.

Harry thought the two were unconnected.

"Personally," Dorothy remarked, "I think Aunt Mary is right. The Green Monster is just a mean joke."

"Danny Rugg could have gotten somebody else to write the note," Nan pointed out.

"I don't know," Bert said. "I have a hunch there *is* a connection between the Green Monster warning and the mystery at Snow Lodge. I can't wait to investigate."

At last, the outline of a large stone house came into view. The roof had a thin crystal-like covering of snow and icicles that dripped from the corners and over the doorway.

"It looks like a gingerbread house!" Flossie exclaimed.

When the family stepped into the living room, they were awed by its enormous size and beauty. One wall was made entirely of stone and had a five-foot-square fireplace above which stretched a wide wooden mantel of walnut. It was the same wood used in the handmade beams that supported the high ceiling. At the far end, overlooking a terrace, were magnificent French doors.

"I wouldn't mind living here at all," Dorothy remarked, admiring the hand-hooked rugs and comfortable leather furnishings.

"Let's start our search for the missing money right after supper," Bert suggested.

"The sooner we unpack, the sooner we eat," Mrs. Bobbsey said.

For the next hour everyone helped unload the van and make the beds. Mrs. Bobbsey put a large casserole dish in the oven. Soon the delicious, golden-baked aroma of Dinah's chicken pot pie filtered into the living room, where a table was set for dinner.

"I think we ought to check out this room first," Bert told Nan.

"And I think you ought to check out this chicken pie before it gets cold," their father interrupted.

But the minute supper was over, Bert again mentioned a tour of the house.

"You all need a good night's sleep," Mrs. Bobbsey said, "so I'm setting a curfew on your detective work. You may search for one hour."

"That's all?" Freddie wailed as Bert took a flashlight from the mantel.

"An hour's plenty of time," Nan replied.

The four older children, followed by Freddie and Flossie, stepped slowly around the spacious living room. They examined the floor for trapdoors and knocked on the paneled walls in quest of secret passageways and hidden openings, but found nothing.

At the end of the fireplace wall was a door. "I wonder where this goes," Dorothy said.

"To the den. That part of the house is only one story high," Freddie explained proudly. "Go on in."

What a fascinating room it was, too! Deerskins, old rifles, powder horns, mounted fish, and a huge moosehead decorated the walls. But despite a careful search, the children found no clues to the missing money.

"Our time's almost up," Nan observed. "Let's take a look in the kitchen."

Nearly one entire side of the kitchen was taken up by a huge walk-in fireplace of stone from which old iron pots hung on hooks.

"Isn't this exciting?" Nan said, stepping into the fireplace and peering up the old chimney. However, as she turned back into the room, she caught sight of an iron ring in the wall. "I wonder—" she mused, and took hold of the rusty ring and pulled.

Slowly a door opened!

"Bert! Dot! Hal!" she called. "I've found something!"

The others came running and crowded in next to her. Cautiously Bert beamed his flashlight into the stony opening. A flight of steps led downward.

"Look!" he cried. "There must be a tunnel underneath this floor!"

At this moment Mrs. Bobbsey came into the kitchen to tell the children their hour was up. "Okay, Mom," Nan said. "We've made a big discovery tonight, and tomorrow we'll find out where this tunnel leads!"

But at breakfast, the children heard a weather forecast and decided to postpone their search until later. "We ought to take a hike before the snow comes," Harry said.

Agreeably, the six children put on their warmest coats, boots, and gloves and climbed to the summit of a large wooded hill not far from the lodge.

"It's fantastic," Dorothy said.

Fields and deep forests, along with scattered houses, met their gaze. In the distance was Lake Metoka, now a broad, flat expanse of ice.

"Let's go over there," Nan proposed.

But as they made their way down the hill again, Bert pointed to a small stone house about a hundred yards from the lodge. "What do you suppose that is?"

Harry went ahead to the run-down structure and pushed open the sagging door. The floor was covered with dirt and the ceiling was high with long hooks hanging from the rafters.

"A smokehouse!" Harry cried. "We used to have one at the farm."

While the boys examined the hooks, Nan and Dorothy rummaged around the floor. Suddenly Dorothy stumbled over something. It was another iron ring.

"I may need help lifting this," Dorothy said, leaning over and grasping the handle firmly. To her surprise, it moved easily and a trapdoor raised up. Below was a flight of steps.

Seeing vague footprints in the dust, Bert exclaimed, "These steps have been used recently! I wonder if this connects with the tunnel starting from the lodge kitchen!"

Nan's eyes sparkled. "Dot and I will go back there and start through the tunnel. You and Hal take this stairway. We'll see if we meet!"

"Good idea. We'll give you five minutes to start."

Followed by Freddie and Flossie, the two older girls charged ahead toward the lodge. They explained their plan to Mrs. Bobbsey. Freddie and Flossie insisted upon going with them.

"Whatever you do, be careful," Mrs. Bobbsey warned as she handed Nan a large flashlight. "Give a holler if you find anything unusual. I'll wait for you here in the kitchen."

"Okay, Mom," Nan said.

"It's so dark!" Dorothy cried, peering over her cousin's shoulder as Nan led the way down the narrow stairway.

Stone walls, glistening with moisture, seemed to press in on the children. Cobwebs spread their silky touch over the young faces, and they heard the scurrying sound of mice.

"It's spooky!" Flossie quavered.

Nan halted, clicked off her flashlight, and held up a hand in warning. "There's a beam of light ahead," she whispered.

"I hope it's Bert and Harry!" Dorothy whispered back.

"I don't see how it could be," Nan said. "They didn't have a flashlight that I know of."

Motionless and silent, the children watched a ray of light play over the walls, the floor, and the ceiling. Gradually the eerie glow moved nearer, and the onlookers felt a cold shudder spread through their bones. The harsh sliver of light flashed across Nan's face.

"Who are you?" Freddie called out bravely.

There was no reply, only a low, scary hiss followed by a moan.

▪ 7 ▪
Cracked Clue

"It *is* you!" Nan cried triumphantly as Harry and Bert rushed forward to join the other children.

"Did you think it was the Green Monster?" her cousin asked.

"To be honest, I wasn't sure," Nan admitted, greatly relieved. "I didn't think you had a flashlight."

"It was awful of you to scare us like that," said Dorothy.

"We thought you could take a joke," said Harry.

"Let's just get out of here," said Flossie.

The searchers returned to the kitchen, thrilled over their discovery. All during lunch they discussed the tunnel. Why had it been constructed to lead from the kitchen to the old smokehouse? And what had it been used for?

"We'll ask Mr. Carford the next time we see him," Nan said eagerly.

"Do you realize it's Christmas Eve?" Bert interjected. "We have a lot to do this afternoon!"

"Like cutting down our Christmas tree," his father said.

Bundling up well and taking an ax from the tool house, Mr. Bobbsey, Bert, Freddie, and Harry set out together.

As soon as they left, Mrs. Bobbsey and the girls began to work on the decorations. Nan and Dorothy strung garlands of fluffy popcorn while Mrs. Bobbsey and Flossie cut fantastic shapes out of posterboard to which they glued silver and gold glitter. Soon the kitchen table was full of tree ornaments.

"Flossie! Look at you!" her mother cried when they were done. The little girl was sprinkled from head to toe with glitter.

"I'm a Christmas-tree ornament!" Flossie exclaimed, spinning around the room until she swooped into a chair.

"That's right," Nan said teasingly. "We'll hang you on the top of the tree, and you can be the Christmas angel!"

"I'd rather be at the bottom where I can open my presents," Flossie said, skipping away to remove the glitter.

A little while later when she returned, the largest spruce tree she had ever seen was standing in a corner of the living room.

"It's bee-yoo-ti-ful, Daddy!" Flossie cried.

"This really is going to be an old-fashioned Christmas." Nan sighed happily.

After the ornaments and strings of popcorn were hung, Dorothy said, "I just had a superior idea!" Grabbing her sweater, she darted outside and came back with an armload of pinecones.

"You are a genius," Nan said excitedly. "We'll put them on the ends of the branches."

By early evening all the decorations were in place and Mrs. Bobbsey sat down contentedly at the piano to play. Soon the air rippled with lively singing.

Only Bert had heard a noise in the kitchen and motioned everyone to stop. Snap, who had been dozing peacefully in front of the fireplace, stood up. His fur bristled as he whimpered and started walking toward the kitchen.

"Lead on, boy!" Nan said, tiptoeing fearlessly after the dog.

Upon reaching the entrance to the kitchen, she stepped inside quickly and gasped. The door in the fireplace was closing.

Nan screamed, instantly bringing the others to her side.

"What's the matter, Nan? Did you see something?" her father asked.

Still trembling, the girl pointed to the fireplace.

"That—that door," she stammered. "I saw it close!"

Waving the rest to stand back, Mr. Bobbsey pulled the iron ring. No one was hiding on the steps.

"Someone bring me a flashlight, please," Mr. Bobbsey said, ordering Snap down the stairs ahead of him.

The dog growled and obeyed. The pair explored the full length of the tunnel ending at the smokehouse door. But there was no evidence of an intruder, and they returned.

"Nan, perhaps you didn't close the fireplace door tightly this morning," her father said. "Then, when you opened the door to the kitchen, a draft forced it shut."

His daughter was unconvinced. "I'm positive someone was in here," Nan said.

"Well, if you're right, dear, we'll make sure no one comes in again," her mother assured her.

She asked the older boys to move a small wooden bench in front of the fireplace door. Mr. Bobbsey then swung one of the huge, heavy iron pots on top of it.

"That ought to do it," said the twins' mother. "Now we'll sing one more carol before you hang up your stockings."

On Christmas morning, Flossie was the first to awaken. She ran from room to room, calling out, "Merry Christmas! Merry Christmas!"

After everyone was assembled, the stocking gifts were opened first. Dorothy gaily pulled out a toy lobster that "pinched" her.

"Santa played a funny joke on you!" Freddie giggled.

Dorothy's frown dissolved into a smile as she tossed the lobster, making it snap again. "I guess I deserve it," she said.

For the next two hours, joyful cries echoed throughout the house. Flossie was especially thrilled with the gift Bert and Nan had made for her—a miniature bed for her doll Susie.

Toward the middle of the afternoon, the children helped serve the turkey dinner. There was so much food that Freddie could hardly finish his plum pudding.

Convinced that everyone was stuffed, Bert brought up the mystery again. Rising lazily to his feet, he said, "Who's ready to hunt? Or am I the only one who needs the exercise?"

"I still think the missing money is near a fireplace," Nan said. "Did anybody happen to count how many there are?"

"Well," Harry began, tapping his cheek, "there's the mantel in the living room, the one in the den, and the one in the kitchen."

"Let's examine the wall around the living-room fireplace," Nan proposed.

"I saw a magnifying glass in the table drawer," Freddie announced, hurrying across the room.

When he returned, the children took turns examining the stones around the mantel.

It was only fifteen minutes later when Nan exclaimed, "I think I've found something!" She pointed to a crack between the mantel and the stone wall.

Bert ran his fingers along the crack and followed it down the side of the fireplace until it disappeared beyond the floorboards.

"May I have the magnifying glass?" Bert requested. "See these little marks?"

"I do!" Dorothy said.

"What are they?" Freddie asked.

"Someone tried to pry open this crack with a chisel!"

"You're right." Nan nodded, bending to study it more closely.

"This is the best clue we've found so far!" Harry declared. "Let me get the flashlight.

Maybe the money dropped down inside."

To their chagrin, however, nothing could be seen. Though disappointed, the twins and their cousins continued to search the fireplace.

"This is getting to be discouraging," Dorothy said. "Maybe we ought to give up."

"Give up?" Nan said. "No way."

The next day, after breakfast, the children took their skates and headed for the lake.

"I want to learn how to make a figure eight," Flossie said as they began skating.

"It's easy," Freddie replied.

"Bert and I will show you," offered Harry while Nan and Dorothy skated back and forth, trying a few fancy moves.

"See," Harry said to the younger twins, "you start off on one foot like this, lean to the—"

Suddenly Freddie stiffened and pointed toward the shoreline. "The Green Monster!" he screamed.

His brother and cousin turned quickly, just in time to see a dark winged figure skim out of sight toward the woods!

"That may have looked like a green monster," Harry said, "but it was *human*!"

"I'm going to track him down and find out who he is!" Bert cried.

"I'm with you," said Harry as Dorothy and Nan joined them.

"You'd better go back to the lodge," Nan told Freddie and Flossie.

"Do we have to?" Freddie whined.

"Yes, you have to. It could be dangerous."

"Come on, Freddie." Flossie took his hand. "It's too cold anyway."

As the four older children picked up their boots and skated across the frozen lake, Freddie and Flossie glanced back.

"I hope the monster doesn't get them," Flossie said.

Just thinking about it made Freddie shiver.

■ 8 ■

On Monster Trail

Nan and Dorothy reached the shoreline ahead of the boys. "Look!" Dorothy exclaimed, pointing to ice-skate-blade prints.

"Find something?" Bert called.

"The monster's trail! Hurry!" Nan said.

She skated toward a trampled spot on the bank, where the phantom creature had evidently paused to remove his skates and put on boots.

"These tracks should be fairly easy to follow," Harry remarked.

After changing into their boots, the four children started inland. On they wandered until they came to an open field where most of the snow had been swept by the wind into a high, icy drift.

"We've lost the bootprints," Nan moaned.

"Maybe not. Let's fan out and take another look," Bert said. But the search, as his sister had predicted, ended in gloomy failure. "We'd better go back."

"I hope you remember where we came in," Dorothy commented, "'cause I sure don't."

Between the fallen branches and snow that lay in a range of peaks along the edge of the field, it was impossible to see any footprints. Around and around the children circled wearily.

Finally, Dorothy hooted, "Over here! I've found the trail back to the lake!"

As they loped after her, none of the travelers realized how far they had gone until Nan practically tripped over a fallen tree trunk. "I can't walk another step!" she panted. "Sorry."

Dorothy flopped down beside her. "My legs hurt too. How about a rest, you guys?" she called out to Bert and Harry.

The boys retraced their steps. "Okay," Bert said, "but it feels like the temperature's dropping. I don't think we should sit too long."

"How about a small fire?" Harry said. "Once we get warmed up, we'll make better time back to the lake. Matches, anybody?"

Bert removed a pack from his coat pocket. "I figured these would come in handy."

"The only thing missing is a nice hot drink," Nan said. "I've got goose bumps!"

"Hang on!" Dorothy said, trotting away.

While the others scattered to collect dead wood for the fire, she fetched a large empty coffee can from under a tree.

She washed the can out with snow, filled it with clean snow, and set it over the low flame. Then she pulled two chocolate bars out of her pocket and broke them into tiny chunks, which she added to the melted contents. Homemade hot chocolate!

In the dry bitter chill, the tasty liquid was warm and comforting. When all of it was gone, the hikers prepared to leave. But then, a few feet away, they heard the sound of snow being crunched underfoot. Was the phantom skater returning?

"Don't move," Bert whispered.

Hardly daring to breathe, the young detectives froze as the heavy footsteps drew nearer. From among the trees a young man emerged. Of medium height, he had plump rosy cheeks and a stocky body that filled out his camouflage jacket.

"Hello, there!" he said. "Are you lost?"

"No, we're on our way back to the lake," Bert replied. "We got tired and decided to stop awhile."

"It's awfully raw out to be sitting in the woods," the stranger said. "My cabin isn't far

from here. Why don't you come back with me. I'll fix you some lunch and show you a fast shortcut to the lake."

"That's very nice of you, Mr.—" Nan replied.

"I'm Dave Burdock. I take hunting parties through the woods," the young man explained.

Stunned, the four children blinked in amazement. *They were actually talking to Mr. Carford's accused nephew!*

Nan was the first to speak. "We've never met, but we—well, we do know your uncle, Mr. Carford. And your aunt Emma Carford, too. In fact, we're spending our Christmas vacation at Snow Lodge."

Hearing Mr. Carford's name, Dave Burdock looked startled.

"I think you know our father, Richard Bobbsey," Nan continued.

"Oh, yes. I'm very glad to meet you. Your father was very good to me a few years ago. But you're not all brothers and sisters, are you?"

The Bobbseys introduced themselves and their cousins. No one mentioned the missing money, however.

"Here I go again gabbing when I should be taking you to the cabin to warm up," the woodsman said. "Follow me, everyone!"

When the log cabin came into view at last,

plumes of smoke were rising out of the chimney. "See? I told you it wasn't far," he said.

"This is so nice of you!" Dorothy said as Dave opened the front door.

"We really appreciate it," Harry added, rubbing his hands in front of the fire. Dave disappeared into the kitchen.

"Can we help?" Nan asked.

"No, thanks. I'll be back before you can catch two squirrels and a robin."

"We couldn't do that until next spring," Nan said, chuckling.

"I always like to give myself plenty of time," the young man said with a smile.

In what seemed like mere seconds he brought a tray with five steaming bowls of vegetable soup and a basket of sesame rolls, which the visitors ate hungrily in between talk of Snow Lodge.

"I hate that place!" Dave muttered angrily.

"Because of the missing money?" blurted Nan.

"We might as well tell you. Dad told us the whole story," Bert said, "and we've been trying to find the money for you. No one really believes you took it!"

"My uncle believes it," Dave said.

"But I'm sure he doesn't," Nan insisted. "He looks so unhappy. I know he'd like to be friends with you again, if only you'd give him half a chance."

"Well, I can't forget the way he treated me or the awful things he said," Dave went on bitterly. "I'll never speak to him until I find that money and prove that I didn't take it!"

"If anyone can help you," Harry said, "my cousins can. They've solved lots of mysteries."

His listener did not seem the least bit interested, which prompted Nan and Bert to talk about the work they had already done. When they mentioned the discovery of the trapdoors and the secret tunnel, Dave was noticeably impressed.

"You must be good detectives," he said. "I lived at Snow Lodge a long time before I found that tunnel."

The twins blushed. "We'll let you know when we find the money," Bert said.

"You do that," Dave replied. Then he showed the twins and their cousins the shortcut back to the lake.

When they were out of earshot, Harry said, "You mean *if* we find the money, Bert."

"We *have to* find it! We want to help clear Dave's name, don't we?"

"Of course we do," Dorothy said.

They followed the winding trail through deep

woods until they recognized the shoreline and returned swiftly to the lodge.

"Did you find the Green Monster?" Freddie shouted as they came up the snowy path.

"No, but we met Dave Burdock!" Nan announced.

"You did!" Freddie exclaimed, running to tell Flossie.

Soon the four children were describing their adventure in the woods, how they had met Dave and had gone to his cabin.

"I feel sorry for him, Mom!" Nan exclaimed. "He's so angry about what happened."

"Maybe you'll be able to find the money for him," Mrs. Bobbsey said soothingly. "You ought to keep trying, anyway."

"Oh, we will," Nan said.

But while most of the afternoon was spent tapping on walls behind the fireplaces, nothing of importance was discovered.

"Zero clues," Dorothy moaned. "Imagine, zero!"

"The mark of a good detective, Dorothy, is persistence," said her aunt.

Soon it was dinnertime. Everyone noticed that Mr. Bobbsey did not eat with his usual gusto.

When dessert was served, he pushed aside his piece of apple pie and gazed absently at the crackling logs.

"You've hardly touched your pie, Dick. What's wrong?" his wife asked.

"Snap's missing. I haven't seen him around since breakfast!"

"But Snap never runs away," Bert said. "Maybe he went to hunt for us."

"That's it!" Nan exclaimed.

Hoping the twins were right, Mr. Bobbsey and the older children trooped off into the cloudy night. They covered nearly half a mile, calling Snap's name and waiting for his gravelly bark. None came.

"We'll have to look for him tomorrow," Mr. Bobbsey decided.

"Oh, no, Dad," Nan pleaded. "What if he's hurt?"

"It's no use, honey. It's too dark and much too cold now." Her father tugged at his scarf, pulling it up to his chin. "We'll just have to say a prayer that Snap is safe."

Blowing hard, the wind lashed out at the searchers as they plodded heartbroken back to the lodge.

∎ 9 ∎

Dog Hero

"Maybe Snap followed our trail to Dave's cabin," Harry said to the twins. "He could be there right now. Snap has an I.D. tag, doesn't he?"

Nan nodded anxiously.

"So Dave will know Snap belongs to you," Dorothy added, "and bring him back tomorrow."

But despite the children's hopes, the beloved pet remained missing the next morning.

"Why don't we go over to Dave's and tell him about Snap?" Dorothy suggested. "If Dave hasn't seen Snap, maybe we can all look together."

Nan, who had slept little the night before, sluggishly pulled on her coat and followed the others across the frosted sun-splashed valley. When they reached the young man's cabin, no one was there.

After a while, Nan shouted, "Here comes Dave now!"

A load of firewood in his arms and whistling cheerily, Dave stepped into view from behind the cabin. "Good morning," he said. "What can I do for you today?"

Bert introduced Freddie and Flossie and told Dave about Snap's sudden disappearance. "We thought maybe he followed us here yesterday."

"Sorry, kids. I haven't seen any dog around here lately, but I'd be glad to help you look."

Together they all scouted the woods surrounding the Burdock cabin but found no paw prints.

"We'll never find Snap," Flossie said tearfully.

"Yes, we will," asserted Freddie. "We'll just keep looking until we do!"

"I wish I could stay a little longer," Dave said, glancing at his watch. "But I have to meet a group of hunters in town. Good luck."

Thanking Dave, the group headed back to shore. As they rounded a wooded bend, they saw a middle-aged man in a parka and jeans coming toward them. Clutching his hand was a small child in a bright-red snowsuit. She was sobbing.

Impulsively, Flossie ran toward her. "Don't cry," she said to the little girl.

"Her collie pup wandered off again," the man explained.

"We're looking for a lost dog, too," Flossie answered.

Bert told what had happened, adding that they were all staying at Snow Lodge.

"So you're the ones!" the man said brightly. "My name's Hoke. I take care of the place for Mr. Carford. My farm's about a mile down the shore toward Lakeport. Hope you found everything in order."

"Oh, yes, Mr. Hoke, everything," Nan said.

"This here is my daughter, Pam."

She glanced shyly at the children through eyes brimming with tears. "H-hello," she stumbled.

"Tell us what your puppy looks like," Dorothy said.

The little girl stared wistfully. "Well, he's kind of yellowish-brown—and fat—and he has a white spot on his chest and a long white mark on his nose. His name is Chipper." She sniffled, ready to burst into tears again.

Flossie stood close to her while Bert began to whistle as he often did when he called Snap. Harry joined in along with Dorothy and Nan.

"I hear barking!" Freddie cried. Everyone stopped and listened to the muffled joyful sound that rang through the frosty air. "That's Snap! Here, boy, here!" Freddie called.

Mr. Hoke and Pam followed the Bobbseys and their cousins to a grove of pines some distance from the path. Afraid the dog was hurt, Bert overtook Freddie.

"Here he is!" the older boy exclaimed. He pointed to a deep pit in the center of the grove.

At the bottom of the hole Snap was jumping and wagging his tail furiously.

"He's hiding something," Nan said.

"Chipper!" screamed Pam Hoke, almost sliding into the hole herself.

The farmer climbed down and, with the help of Bert and Harry, lifted the animals out. Pam and Flossie were laughing and crying at the same time. Afterward, the children tried to reconstruct what had happened.

"I'll bet Chipper fell into the hole and couldn't get out," Nan began.

"And Snap was on his way to find us," Bert continued, "but heard the puppy yelping and went to rescue him. Then he discovered he couldn't carry Chipper and climb out of the hole, too."

"So he stayed with the puppy to keep him safe and warm!" Harry concluded.

"What a brave dog!" Dorothy smiled.

Hearing all of this, Pam threw her arms around Snap's neck and hugged him gratefully. "You're a real hero, Snap! You saved Chipper!"

"Well, my friends," the farmer said, shaking hands with all of the children, "Pam and I are deeply thankful, I must say, especially to you, Snap."

Barking as if to say "You're welcome," Snap ambled over to Chipper and licked the puppy good-bye.

The children said good-bye too, and set off once again for Snow Lodge. Laughing and singing happily on the way, they were surprised to meet Dave Burdock.

"I decided to postpone my trip into town," he said. "I thought maybe I'd take another look around for Snap, but I see you found him. Where was he?"

Proudly Flossie and Freddie related the story of Snap's heroism.

"Dave," Nan interrupted, "why don't you come back to Snow Lodge with us. I know my Dad would like to see you again."

Dave's face clouded. "I can't, but thanks anyway," he said.

"You tried," Bert murmured to Nan as Snap nuzzled against her.

At the lodge, after the children fed Snap, they

reported the day's events to Mr. and Mrs. Bobbsey. "Dave wouldn't come back with us," Nan added glumly.

"It's too bad he's so resentful and stubborn," her father said. "Dave and Mr. Carford could be living here right now."

"Finding the money would solve everything," Bert said. "Let's do it."

Organizing yet another hunt, the young detectives searched with renewed enthusiasm, but by bedtime they had still found nothing.

"Maybe we can talk Dave into forgiving his uncle," Bert proposed.

"You heard Dad. Dave is too stubborn," Nan said. "I have another idea. Tomorrow, let's go through the tunnel and examine every inch of it one more time."

Following the girl's suggestion, after sunup the children put on their warmest clothes, armed themselves with flashlights, and stepped through the secret door in the kitchen fireplace. Bert took the lead with Dorothy, Flossie, and Nan behind him, followed by Freddie and Harry in the rear.

As they flashed their lights over the brick walls and ceiling, they realized the passageway was larger than they had thought. At least three feet wide, it was spacious enough to permit a six-foot man to walk through upright.

"I wonder how old this tunnel is," Bert said.

"It's *very* old," Flossie said, trembling.

"Halt, everybody!" Bert commanded, bending forward suddenly.

Dorothy nearly crashed into him. "What is it?" she asked.

Nan pressed closer to see.

"A black coat button! And I don't think it has been here very long!"

Bert turned it over in his fingers. The button was still shiny. "Someone has been down here recently!" he said.

"So I was right!" Nan exclaimed. "I knew it wasn't the wind that made the door in the fireplace close on Christmas Eve. It was a real live person!"

■ 10 ■
Enemy Friend

As the six detectives gaped in surprise at the black button, Dorothy asked, "Why would anyone be using this tunnel now?"

"I wish I knew." Nan shrugged. "Looks like we'd better be ready for anything—"

"And anyone," her cousin said grimly.

The rest of the search proved uneventful, however. When they reached the stairs and trapdoor leading to the smokehouse, they had found no further clues to the mysterious intruder and stepped hurriedly into the sunlight.

"Whew! Am I glad to be out of there!" Flossie declared. "Let's go see Mr. Burdock."

The children labored through the crusty snow until they came within sight of the familiar cabin. Small puffs of smoke rose from the chimney.

They ran forward, and Bert knocked on the

door. No one answered. "Maybe he went into town," Freddie said.

"And left a fire burning in the fireplace?" Nan said doubtfully. "Let's check the door. If it's unlocked, I vote we go in. Dave could be hurt."

Reluctantly, Bert pulled the knob, and the door creaked open, revealing a hastily made cot.

"He could be in the kitchen," Harry said. Then he called out, "Dave? Are you here?" Again there was no answer.

Bewildered, Nan walked to the cot to sit down. To her shock, sticking out from behind it was something thick and green. "Oh, no!" she cried, dragging out the garment.

It was a green cape!

"That's what the Green Monster wears!" Freddie exclaimed.

"Dave Burdock is the Green Monster? No!" Dorothy said.

"The top button on the cape is missing," Bert observed. From his pocket he took the button he had found in the tunnel of Snow Lodge. "It matches perfectly. I hate to say it, but it looks as if Dave has been spying on us."

"You don't really think Mr. Carford's nephew is the Green Monster, do you?" Nan asked. "It doesn't make sense."

"But he is," Harry concluded indignantly.

At this moment Nan happened to glance out the window. Dave Burdock and another man, wearing a dark-blue ski cap and jacket, were walking toward the cabin.

"He's coming," Nan said. "Keep cool, everybody."

"Well—visitors," Dave said, opening the door. "I didn't expect to see you here today."

The children did not smile, and Freddie charged forward in his most accusing voice. "You're the Green Monster!"

"What!" Dave exclaimed.

"This is your cape," Harry told him, holding it up, "the one you wear to hide under."

Speechless, Dave Burdock stared blankly at the garment. "I never saw that before in my life," he said, turning to his companion. "Will, do you—"

But Will was already streaking up the path. Diving after him, Bert, Harry, and Dave caught up to him and grabbed the fleeing man and marched him back to the cabin.

"Now, suppose you tell me what's going on here," Dave demanded.

Will stood bleakly silent, prompting Bert to tell about the warning note to the Bobbsey Twins and the stranger who had secretly visited Snow Lodge.

"Okay, I might as well talk," the man grumbled.

He told the Bobbseys his name was Will Beck and, like Dave, he was a woodsman. "I've known the old man and Dave here for a long time. I believed Dave's story about the money, and I figured I'd try my hand at finding it.

"When I heard from the Hokes that you were coming to the lodge—well, I didn't want you snooping around and finding it before me."

"What difference does it make who finds the money," Bert interrupted, "so long as Mr. Carford gets it back?"

"He don't deserve it!" Will sputtered.

"You mean you were planning to keep it for yourself?" Harry burst out.

"I was going to split it with Dave. He's my friend."

"But the money, if it's ever found, belongs to my uncle," Dave said.

"That mean old codger? Bah!" Will scoffed.

"He's very kind—a regular Santa Claus," Nan spoke up.

"I'd like to know why you called yourself the Green Monster and wore the cape," Dorothy asked.

"To keep people from seeing my face and to scare you if I could," Will explained, wringing his hands nervously. "My father used to wear this cape in the woods when it was cold, so that's where I got the idea. The only wrong I did was to call myself the Green Monster. Dave didn't know a thing about it."

As the questioning continued, Will also admitted phoning the Bobbseys' home and pretending to be an employee of the *Lakeport News*. "I wanted to find out when you'd all be at the lodge."

"I'm amazed at you, Will Beck. You've always been honest and straightforward. I hope this has been a lesson to you."

"I'm sorry, Dave," Will said.

Saying no more, he picked up his cape, took the missing button from Bert, and stalked sheepishly out the door.

"Oh, I'm so glad you weren't the Green Monster!" Flossie said, rushing to hug the young woodsman.

"At least nobody mean found the money at Snow Lodge," Freddie put in. "Now we can hunt even harder!"

"And that's just what we plan to do!" Nan said assuringly.

"Assuming we get home before the next blizzard," Dorothy said. She was gazing up at the darkened sky as fine flakes of snow swirled over the ground. "We'd better hurry."

"Come on, Floss. I'll give you a ride on my back," Bert said.

"You hop on, too, Freddie," Harry offered.

The younger twins squealed happily as Nan and Dorothy pushed ahead through the thickening snow. "It's getting windier," Dorothy said, her face buried deep in her collar.

About a hundred yards beyond the shoreline, they glimpsed the lights of the lodge. "Hold on, Floss!" Bert yelled over the howling wind.

Using every ounce of strength, the children raced toward Snow Lodge. But then a gust struck and knocked them about.

"Don't let go!" Bert shouted again.

"I'm falling!" his little sister wailed. "Help!" Her mittened fingers slid off her brother's shoulders as another gust whipped her over backward. Instantly Nan leapt forward to catch the hood of Flossie's snowsuit as Bert picked her up in his arms and staggered slowly toward the lodge.

Harry, who still had Freddie in tow, arrived first and threw open the door for Nan and Dorothy.

"Hurry!" they cried to Bert, watching him reel against the harsh, blustery wind.

Minutes later, when he and Flossie were finally safe inside, Mr. and Mrs. Bobbsey shoved the door back and latched it firmly shut.

"Take off those wet clothes right away and sit by the fire," the twins' mother said. "We want to hear everything that happened."

Excitedly the young detectives told of their latest discovery. "That's quite a story, kids," Mr. Bobbsey said. "For a while you almost had me convinced there really was a green monster. I'm glad that mystery is solved."

As he spoke, the room grew dimmer from the darkness outside, and Mrs. Bobbsey switched on more lights. They flickered, then went out entirely.

"Just what we don't need—a power failure," Bert said, peering disgustedly out a window.

"Between the wind and the weight of the snow," Mr. Bobbsey said, "a wire was bound to come down. We'll probably be without electricity for quite a while."

Candles were lit along with kerosene lamps that Mr. Bobbsey found in the cellar.

"I'm glad Mr. Carford didn't get rid of the old wood-burning stove in the kitchen after he installed a modern electric range," Mrs. Bobbsey remarked.

As the afternoon wore on, the children became restless. They had searched carefully for the money downstairs and concluded it must be somewhere else.

"Maybe we should try the attic," Nan said.

With Bert and Harry each carrying a lantern, the six children mounted the stairs, at the top of which was another short flight. They climbed this last flight and entered the attic. Against the attic wall were several dusty-looking trunks.

Nan raised the lid of the nearest trunk and removed several old-fashioned suits and dresses, under which were fancy satin shoes with little tassels on them.

"Let's all dress up!" Dorothy exclaimed.

Flossie, meanwhile, had stooped to pick up a leather pouch that had fallen out of the folds of clothing. "What's this?" she asked.

"What's what?" Nan responded.

"This." The little girl held the pouch up for everyone to see.

"Open it!" Dorothy exclaimed.

Flossie's chubby fingers pulled at the flap, causing it to spring open upside down. A flood of bills came pouring out. "It's Mr. Carford's money!"

▪ 11 ▪

Snowbound

Everyone watched as Flossie collected the money and Bert counted it.

"This can't be what we're looking for," he said.

"It isn't Mr. Carford's money?" Freddie asked in bewilderment.

"Yes it is, but it's not much."

"Hardly enough to cause a rift between Dave and his uncle," Nan pointed out.

"Even so, I'm sure Mr. Carford will be glad to get it back," Harry said. Snatching up a pair of long tight trousers and a ruffled shirt from the trunk, he added, "I'll drop these off in my room and then tell Aunt Mary and Uncle Dick about the money. See you in a couple of minutes."

Soon the other children each had an armful of clothes that they carried to their rooms to try on. When they reappeared, Mr. and Mrs. Bobbsey were reading in front of the fire.

Nan and Dorothy wore crinolines that swayed as they walked, showing white frilly pantalets underneath. Flossie had on a long green skirt tied up under her arms with a big red sash. Careful not to trip, she shuffled along, mimicking the older boys in their oversized trousers and tailcoats. Freddie strode in last, wearing cowboy chaps, with a toy lariat draped from his belt.

"What a fashion show!" Mrs. Bobbsey said, applauding while her husband went to get his camera.

"May we have a party later?" Nan asked her mother.

"We'll take care of everything, Aunt Mary," Dorothy promised. "All you have to do is come and have fun with us."

"Sounds good to me," Mrs. Bobbsey replied, winking as her husband snapped a picture.

For the rest of the afternoon the six playmates forgot about the snowstorm. Nan and Dorothy made party sandwiches and baked cupcakes in the old-fashioned wood-burning stove while Bert and Harry planned skits and games.

When everything was done, Dorothy discovered the younger twins whispering in secret. "What are you two planning?"

"Oh—uh—nothing," Freddie replied, squirming. Giggling, he and Flossie disappeared up the stairs.

After supper, Mr. and Mrs. Bobbsey also vanished without a word.

"What happened to Aunt Mary and Uncle Dick?" Dorothy asked as the cousins assembled in the living room.

Then they heard a *swish* coming from the hallway, and a quaintly dressed couple entered arm in arm.

"Surprise!" Mr. and Mrs. Bobbsey exclaimed.

"We thought we should dress formally for your party," Mrs. Bobbsey added.

"You look spectacular, Aunt Mary!" Dorothy said, admiring her aunt's flowing blue-silk gown and large organza hat wreathed in flowers.

"Thank you, Dorothy."

"Daddy, you're bee-yoo-ti-ful, too!" Flossie said.

Wearing narrow striped trousers, a gold brocaded vest, and long black jacket, Flossie's father carried a tall silk hat and gold-handled cane.

"You looked so cute we decided to see what else was in those trunks," he said.

"How about something to eat?" Freddie piped up.

"You're the boss," Dorothy said, smiling.

As soon as she and Nan brought in the dainty

sandwiches and cupcakes, Flossie and Freddie put a fancy paper hat on each of the children.

Their plates heaped with food, the younger children went to a corner of the living room where pillows had been arranged in front of a makeshift stage.

"Why don't you sit with us by the fire?" Mrs. Bobbsey said after the pair had become unusually quiet.

No reply came, and she glanced across the room. Freddie, still clutching his half-eaten cupcake, was fast asleep, with Flossie beside him.

"Let's put them to bed, Dick," Mrs. Bobbsey said. "I thought this might happen."

But as Freddie was lifted from the pillows, his eyes flashed wide open. "Hi, Daddy! We're all ready for the skits."

"The skits can wait until tomorrow. You two are pretty sleepy, and it's past your bedtime."

"I wasn't really sleeping," Freddie insisted groggily. "Please, Daddy. Can't we do our skits?"

"All right, but then you must go to bed."

As Freddie and Flossie sped out of the room, Harry grinned. "I saw him making paste out of flour and water."

"And Flossie asked me to tie two big red hair ribbons together. I wonder what they're up to," Nan said.

"Okay, we're ready!" Freddie called. "Are you ready?"

"We're ready," Bert said, settling back on a pillow next to Harry.

"Here we come!" Flossie exclaimed.

Her lips parted in a mischievous grin, Flossie strolled into view dressed only in underwear, with a huge red ribbon draped across one shoulder and fastened at her hip in a bow.

The audience laughed loudly.

"Brrr!" said Nan to Flossie. "Aren't you cold?"

Freddie came next. He wore a beard made out of cotton that was pasted together with flour and water, and his small body was wrapped in a large sheet, held together at the waist by a safety pin.

"Do you know who we are?" he asked, smirking as he held up an hourglass egg timer.

"Snow White and Prince Charming?" his father guessed.

Flossie giggled. "No."

"Jack and Jill?" Bert said.

"We'll have to tell them, Freddie," Flossie said with a sigh.

"I'm Father Time," the boy announced. "And Flossie's Baby New Year!"

Clapping heartily with the others, Nan said, "We knew who you were the whole time."

94

"You did?" Freddie replied.

"Your skit was great," Harry congratulated his cousins.

No sooner had he finished speaking than an ear-piercing snap, like the sound of a giant whip cracking over timber, split the air.

"What was that?" Flossie asked, running to her mother.

Next came an ominous crash that thundered across the room, causing Snow Lodge to shudder on its foundation. Bits of mortar spewed from the fireplace onto the floor as heavy wind mixed with snow blew out of the den, engulfing the family.

"A tree must've hit the roof," Mr. Bobbsey said, dashing toward the room.

Indeed, a massive tree had fallen directly over the den. The uppermost branches blocked the entry from the living room while snow-laden boughs lay heavily on the crushed furniture. Even the old fireplace was partially demolished. Its long heavy mantelpiece rested sideways on the floor.

"We've got to close this whole area off," Mr. Bobbsey said. "I'll get an ax from the cellar."

When he returned, he instructed Harry and Bert to lift aside some of the smaller branches. It seemed hours before enough of the tree

trunk could be removed and the door shut. Still, cold air seeped through the sagging frame.

"Now what'll we do?" Mrs. Bobbsey asked.

While she and her husband talked out of earshot of the children, Harry went to the kitchen for rags and newspapers and stuffed them around the door.

"That ought to help for a little while, anyway," he said.

"As soon as everything's cleaned up," Mr. Bobbsey spoke, "I'm going to get a progress report on our furnace. I don't want to stay here any longer than necessary."

The six detectives crumbled in despair.

"Why such long faces?"

"We haven't found Mr. Carford's money yet," said Nan, "and if we have to leave soon, we might never find it!"

▪ 12 ▪

Happy Reunion

Mr. Bobbsey barely heard the answer as he rechecked the frame of the door yet another time.

"Dad?" Bert said, "Do we have to leave right away?"

"If it were possible, which it isn't," his father said, satisfied that all the gaps were plugged securely, "I'd say yes."

"Does that mean we can stay until we find the money and get Mr. Carford and Dave back together?" Dorothy asked.

Mr. Bobbsey gazed into the children's pleading eyes but said nothing.

"At the moment," the twins' mother said, "we're more concerned about your safety."

Mr. Bobbsey, who had started to examine the rest of the adjoining wall, stopped long enough to look out the window. "I can't even see the road," he said. "Talk about being snowbound."

"Yippee! We're stuck!" Harry chortled.

"Hooray! Hooray!" Dorothy cried.

"I imagine a plow will come through as soon as the storm's over," Mrs. Bobbsey said.

"If we're lucky," Nan whispered to her cousins, "it won't be before late tomorrow."

Surveying the mountain of mortar chips and stone from the living-room wall, Bert and Harry grabbed brooms and swept the debris into a corner.

"We'll have to get rid of this in the morning," Mrs. Bobbsey remarked. "Okay, troops, follow me." She picked up one of the kerosene lamps and led the children upstairs to their rooms.

The next day, bright golden sunshine filtered through Freddie's window.

"Yahoo!" he cried, bolting into the hallway. "Wake up, Flossie! Wake up, Nan!"

Running to the stairway, Freddie flew down the steps to inspect the damage. "What a mess!" he declared as the rest of the household descended, yawning.

His father organized work crews to begin removal of the debris. While he and Bert sawed off tree limbs, the other children went out to shovel snow.

"Make two paths, if you can," Mr. Bobbsey

said, "one to the woodpile and the other to the road."

"Will do, Uncle Dick," Harry said.

Both tasks were completed by noon, and the four older cousins helped carry the tree limbs outside.

"It looks worse than I thought," Mrs. Bobbsey said, staring up at the gash in the ceiling. "We'd better move what's left of the good furniture along with the books and knickknacks into other rooms. Be careful. Take only a little at a time, please."

All hands set to work willingly transferring the articles. Bert stacked a tall pile of books in Flossie's arms, causing her to sway back on her feet.

"Whoops!" Flossie cried. First one book slid to the floor, then the entire column of books, followed by the little girl herself as she whirled around to catch them. "I'm sorry, Mommy."

"It was my fault, Mom," Bert apologized, helping Flossie to her feet.

As he knelt to pick up the books, he noticed Nan peering into a crack of loosened mortar in back of where the mantelpiece had been.

"Come here, everybody!" she said excitedly. "I see something. Could it be—"

The other children crowded around her.

Bert, Harry, and Dorothy as well as Nan tried sliding their hands through the opening but with little success.

"You try it, Floss," Bert said, lifting her up.

Flossie twisted her small hand into the crack easily. "I feel something!" she declared.

The children held their breaths. "Is it money?" Dorothy asked.

"I'm not sure. Could be," Flossie said, stretching deeper into the hole and pulling out a narrow stack of papers.

They were old, dusty bills, all for large amounts of money. Dumbstruck, the group hurried into the living room, where Mr. and Mrs. Bobbsey were rearranging furniture.

"We've found it!" Bert exclaimed as Flossie waved the bills in the air. "The missing money! See, Dave didn't steal it! And Will didn't find it!"

Mr. Bobbsey counted the money. "It's the exact amount that Mr. Carford said he lost. It must have slipped behind the mantel somehow."

"And to think it was here all the time!" Nan said. "Poor Dave and poor Mr. Carford!"

After the trouble that had befallen Snow Lodge, it was now a scene of happiness.

"Actually," said Nan, "the storm and falling tree were blessings in disguise."

"If you hadn't been on the lookout, dear,"

Mrs. Bobbsey said, "the money might have gone unnoticed."

"It probably would have stayed right where it was and been covered over by a new mantel," Mr. Bobbsey noted.

"We ought to tell Dave and Mr. Carford right away," Bert interjected.

"Dave first," replied his dad.

But as they discussed hiking to the young man's cabin, there was an unexpected knock at the back door.

"I'll get it," Freddie said, skipping to the kitchen. "Dave!"

"How're you doing?" Dave asked.

"We found it!"

"Found it?" Dave repeated.

"Yes!" Freddie exclaimed, jumping up and down.

"Whoa, slow down, tiger! What exactly did you find?"

Before the boy could explain, the other children assembled around him.

"Isn't it great? Isn't it great?" Dorothy chattered gaily.

"I'm sure it is, but—" Dave began.

"We found it behind the mantelpiece. How about that?" Nan said as Flossie displayed the money.

"Isn't it exciting!" Flossie said, giggling.

Overwhelmed by emotion, Dave followed the twins into the living room. "I don't know how to thank you. It's a miracle," he said, sinking into a chair. "A real miracle."

"I'm very happy for you," Mr. Bobbsey said.

"I want to tell my uncle immediately," Dave replied.

"I can't blame you," said Mr. Bobbsey. "But I'm afraid we're also going to have to tell him about the tree that fell through the den roof. I guess you couldn't see it from the back door."

"No," said Dave, holding his head in dismay.

"I'm sure the other news will be far more important to him." Mr. Bobbsey paused. Then he said, "By the way, do you know how the road is to Lakeport?"

"That's why I came over here, to tell you the plows have been running all morning," Dave said. "The road's clear, and they say electricity will be restored soon."

"Good enough. Then I'll go," Mr. Bobbsey said.

"How about bringing Mr. Carford back with you?" Bert proposed.

"That's a wonderful idea," his mother said.

"I haven't seen my uncle in such a long time," Dave commented. "I won't know what to say."

"Just say hello," Flossie said, snuggling under the young man's arm.

Dave patted her on the head. "I guess that is the best way to start," he said.

Soon Mr. Bobbsey departed, leaving Dave behind to help bring in wood for the fireplace. Before dark, however, power was restored, the kerosene lamps were returned to the basement, and the Bobbsey van swung into the driveway with Mr. Carford.

He strode toward his nephew, both hands extended. "Dave," his voice trembled, "I hope you can find it in your heart to forgive me for the terrible, terrible things I said to you. I know I accused you unjustly."

Dave cleared his throat.

Mr. Carford continued, "For a long time now I've felt you couldn't have been guilty, but you refused to see me or talk to me."

"I know, and I'm sorry, Uncle Jess," Dave murmured. "I wish none of this had ever happened."

"So do I. Now that the money has been found, can't we please be friends again?"

Dave flushed in embarrassment and grasped his uncle's hands. "I'd like that very much. It's what I've been hoping for. Let's never—never fight again."

As everyone sat down to dinner, Mr. Carford

had a broad, contented smile on his face. "This is the best way I know of to begin a new year!"

"And we owe it all to the Bobbseys. You kids are really super!" Dave said.

"Perhaps you'll learn something from all of this too," Mr. Carford said to the children. "Never accuse anyone of wrongdoing unless you are absolutely sure."

His listeners were thoughtfully silent for several minutes. "Mr. Carford, what if we're pretty sure?" Flossie asked.

"Not pretty sure. Absolutely positive," the elderly man replied.

"Santa Flossie has an extra present for you too," the little girl said, giving him the leather pouch.

"It's full of money," Freddie added.

"My goodness, another lost treasure!" Mr. Carford replied. "Thank you, Santa Flossie."

"You're welcome," she said as the other children related all their adventures at the lodge. Presently Nan asked if the owner knew about the tunnel leading from the kitchen to the old smokehouse.

"I haven't thought about it in years. I used to play in it sometimes when I was a boy."

"We were wondering how old the tunnel is," Bert said. "And what it was used for."

"I can't give you any precise dates, but it has to be well over two hundred years old. I know this house went up before the American Revolution. The farmer who built it probably used the tunnel to get from the kitchen to the smokehouse during heavy snowfalls."

"Oh," Flossie said, obviously disappointed that there wasn't more to the intriguing story.

"Of course—" Mr. Carford smiled.

"Of course what?" Flossie encouraged.

"Well, there are rumors that the tunnel was used to hide American soldiers during the Revolutionary War."

"How interesting!" Nan said. "Just think! Maybe one of our ancestors hid down there!"

"Maybe so," the elderly man replied. "The English captured this area early in the war and imprisoned a number of American soldiers nearby. People say some of them managed to escape and lived in the tunnel for weeks at a time.

"Then, when the coast was clear," he continued, "the soldiers would sneak back to their own army."

"I wonder what it was like living in the tunnel," Bert said.

"Probably very cold and very damp," Mr. Bobbsey answered.

Feeling chilled all of a sudden, Freddie

rubbed his arms. "Did the soldiers get sick a lot?" he inquired.

"Oh, I imagine so, but they were a hardy lot, thank goodness," Mr. Carford said.

While he and Freddie speculated further, the other children talked about the part the old tunnel had played in winning the Revolutionary War.

When the discussion was finished, Mrs. Bobbsey proclaimed, "It seems to me the children have solved three mysteries during our stay at Snow Lodge."

"That's right, Aunt Mary," said Dorothy. "The secret tunnel—"

"And the Green Monster mystery," Bert said, glimpsing a wink from Dave.

"And most important, the case of the missing money," Nan added.

"We should go into the mystery-solving business!" Freddie exclaimed.

Conversation buzzed happily as the young detectives tried predicting where their next adventure would take them. They would find out for certain in a most unusual way in *The Bobbsey Twins on a Houseboat.*

"When we get home," Freddie said, "let's hang a sign on our front door that says, 'The Bobbsey Twins' Detective Agency'!"

"*Unlimited!*" Bert added happily.